D0506957

A Piggie Christmas

Howard Fine

Hyperion Books for Piglets
New York

Illustrations copyright © 2000 by Howard Fine

All rights reserved. No part of this book may be
reproduced in any form or by any means, electronic or
mechanical, including photocopying, recording, or by any
information storage and retrieval system, without written
permission from the publisher. For information address
Hyperion Books for Children, 114 Fifth Avenue,
New York, New York 10011-5690.
Printed in Hong Kong
First Edition
1 3 5 7 9 10 8 6 4 2

Library of Congress Cataloging-in-Publication Data
Fine, Howard.
A piggie Christmas / illustrated by Howard Fine.—1st ed.
p. cm.
Summary: A collection of popular Christmas carols in which
the illustrations feature pig characters.
ISBN 0-7868-0587-0 (trade)
1. Carols, English—Texts. 2. Christmas music—Texts. 3. Swine—Songs and music.
[1. Carols. 2. Christmas music. 3. Pigs—Songs and music.] I. Title.

PZ8.3.F616 Pi 2000
782.42'1723—dc21
99-87561 [E]

Visit www.hyperionchildrensbooks.com

For Anne, Ken, and Katherine
—H.F.

— Contents —

The Twelve Days
of Christmas

UP ON THE
HOUSETOP

Jingle Bells

Deck the Halls

We Wish You
a Piggie Christmas

The Twelve Days of Christmas

On the first day of Christmas,
my true love gave to me
a partridge in a pear tree.

On the second day of Christmas,
my true love gave to me
2 turtle doves
and a partridge in a pear tree.

On the third day of Christmas,
my true love gave to me
3 French hens,
2 turtle doves,
and a partridge in a pear tree.

On the fourth day of Christmas, my true love gave to me **4** calling birds,

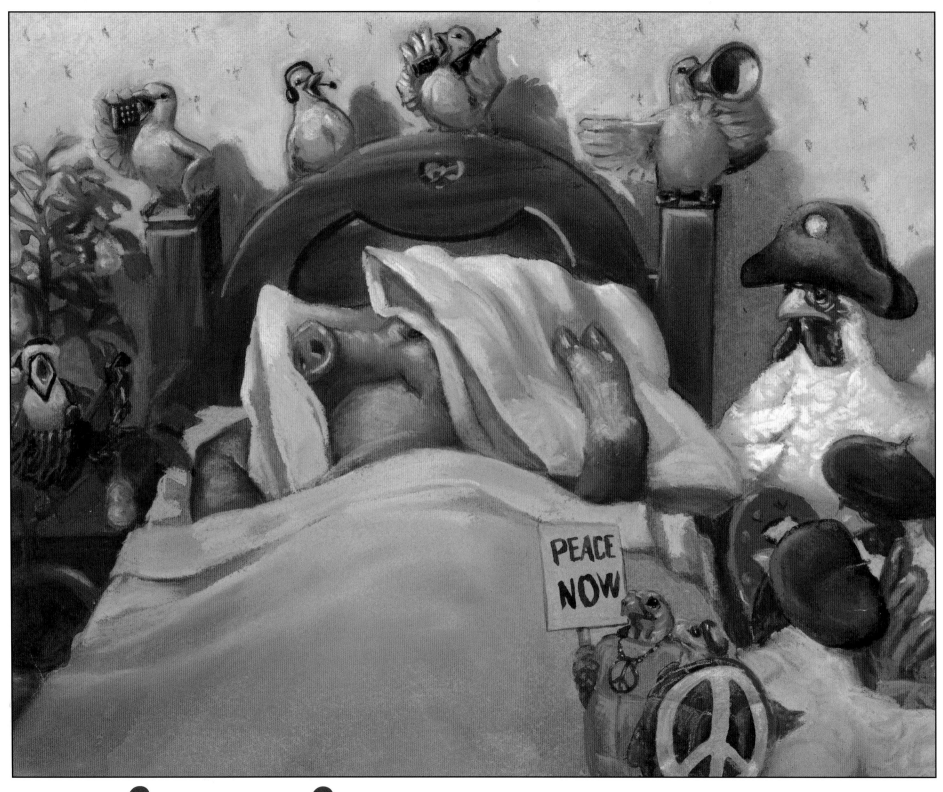

3 French hens, **2** turtle doves, and a partridge in a pear tree.

On the fifth day of Christmas, my true love gave to me **5 GOLDEN RINGS!**

4 calling birds, **3** French hens, **2** turtle doves, and a partridge in a pear tree.

On the sixth day of Christmas, my true love gave to me **6** geese a-laying,

On the seventh day of Christmas, my true love gave to me **7** swans a-swimming,

6 geese a-laying, **5** GOLDEN RINGS! **4** calling birds, **3** French hens,

2 turtle doves, and a partridge in a pear tree.

On the eighth day of Christmas, my true love gave to me **8** maids a-milking,

On the ninth day of Christmas, my true love gave to me 9 ladies dancing,

8 maids a-milking, **7** swans a-swimming, **6** geese a-laying, **5** GOLDEN

RINGS! **4** calling birds, **3** French hens, **2** turtle doves, and a

partridge in a pear tree.

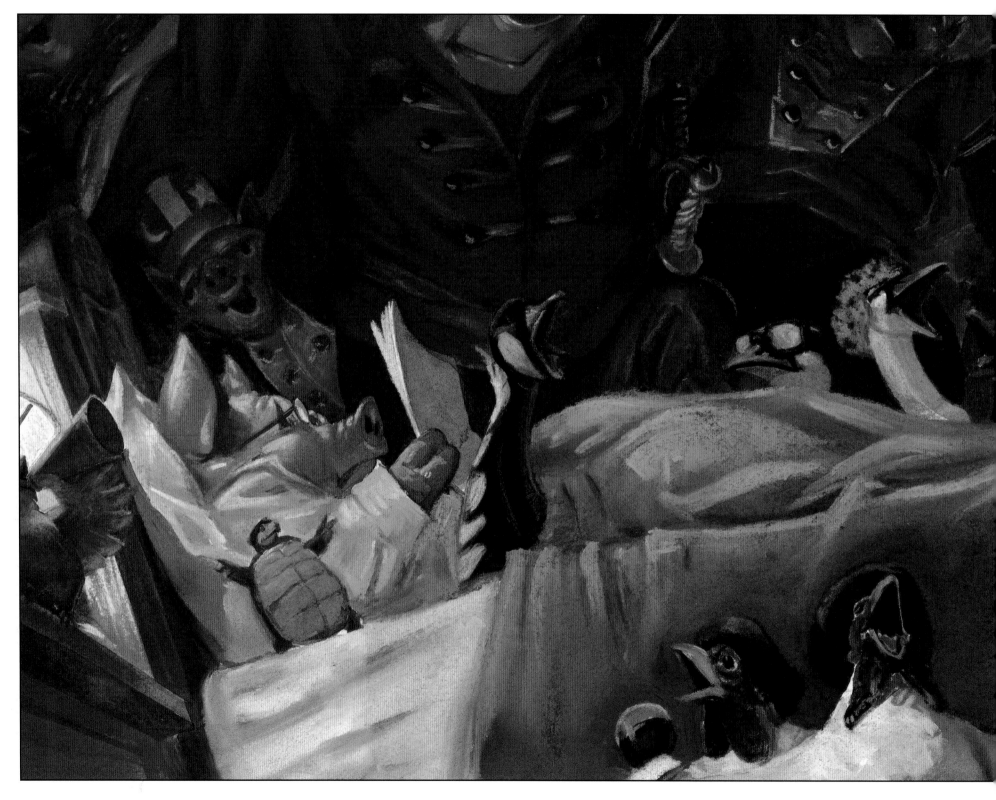

9 ladies dancing, **8** maids a-milking, **7** swans a-swimming, **6** geese a-laying,

5 GOLDEN RINGS! **4** calling birds, **3** French hens,

2 turtle doves, and a partridge in a pear tree.

On the eleventh day of Christmas, my true love gave to me **11** pipers piping,

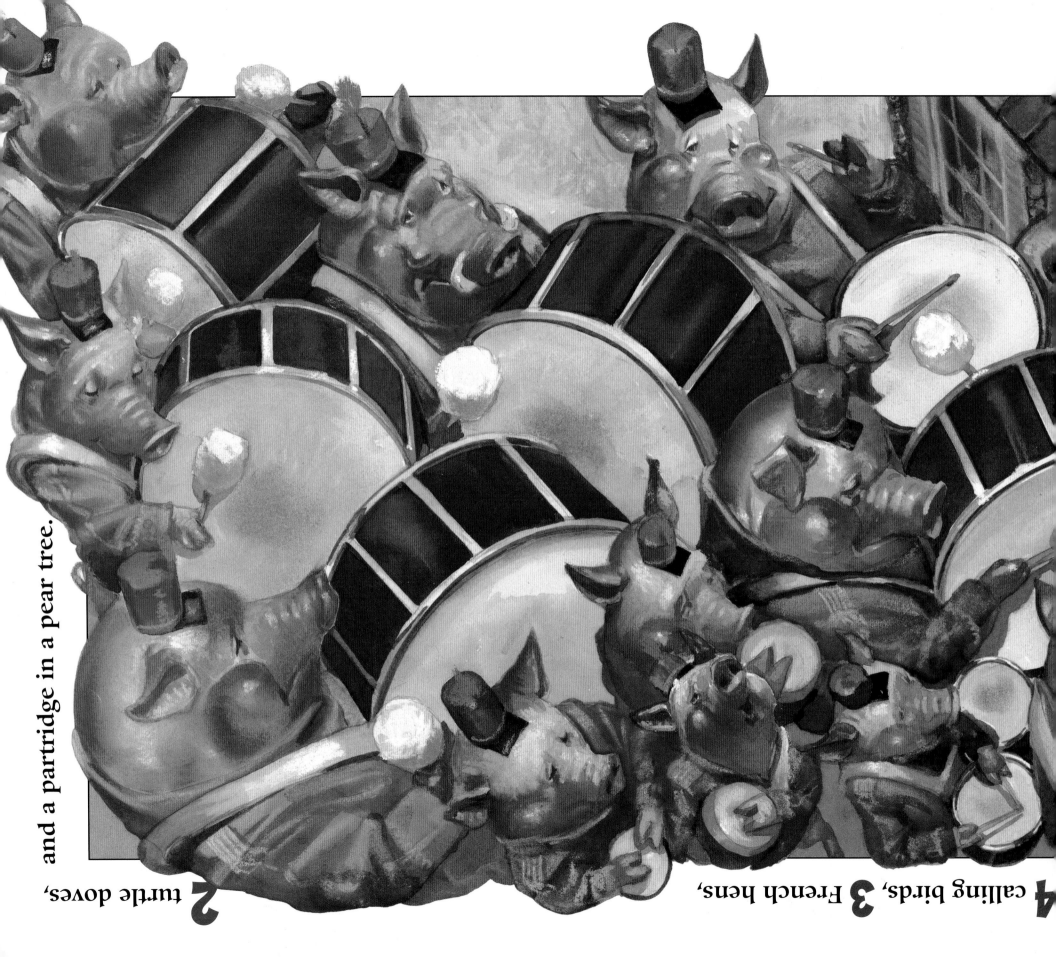

and a partridge in a pear tree.

2 turtle doves,

4 calling birds, **3** French hens,

On the twelfth day of Christmas, my true love gave to me **12** drummers drumming,

11 pipers piping, **10** lords a-leaping, **9** ladies dancing, **8** maids a-milking, **7** swans a-swimming, **6** geese a-laying, **5** GOLDEN RINGS!

UP ON THE HOUSETOP

Up on the housetop reindeer pause,
Out jumps good old Santa Claus;
Down through the chimney with lots of toys,
All for the little ones, Christmas joys.
Ho, ho, ho! Who wouldn't go!
Ho, ho, ho! Who wouldn't go!
Up on the housetop, click, click, click,
Down through the chimney with good Saint Nick.

First comes the stocking of little Nell,

Oh, dear Santa, fill it well.

Give her a dollie that laughs and cries,

One that will open and shut her eyes.

Ho, ho, ho! Who wouldn't go!

Ho, ho, ho! Who wouldn't go!

Up on the housetop, click, click, click,

Down through the chimney with good Saint Nick.

Jingle Bells

Dashing through the snow
In a one-horse open sleigh,
O'er the fields we go,
Laughing all the way;
Bells on Bobtail ring,
Making spirits bright.
What fun it is to ride and sing
A sleighing song tonight!

Jingle bells! Jingle bells!
Jingle all the way!
Oh, what fun it is to ride
In a one-horse open sleigh!
Jingle bells! Jingle bells!
Jingle all the way!
Oh, what fun it is to ride
In a one-horse open sleigh!

Deck the Halls

Deck the halls with boughs of holly,
Fa la la la la, la la la la.
'Tis the season to be jolly,
Fa la la la la, la la la la.
Don we now our gay apparel,
Fa la la, la la la, la la la.
Troll the ancient Yuletide carol.
Fa la la la la, la la la la.

See the blazing yule before us,
Fa la la la la, la la la la.
Strike the harp and join the chorus,
Fa la la la la, la la la la.
Follow me in merry measure,
Fa la la, la la la, la la la.
While I tell of Yuletide treasure.
Fa la la la la, la la la la.

We Wish You a Piggie Christmas

We wish you a Piggie Christmas,

We wish you a Piggie Christmas,

We wish you a Piggie Christmas,

And a Happy New Year!